Funny Business

An Anthology of Humor

Contents

10 Things
Your Parents Will Never Say

Steven Herrick *Illustrated by Mitch Vane*

1.  Let's forget dinner tonight; we'll eat ice cream instead.

2. Goodnight children, I'm off to bed. Stay up as late as you want.

3.  No homework tonight. You are absolutely forbidden to do homework.

4. Yes, of course you can have 21 of your friends over to stay on Saturday night. We've got lots of room.

5. Children, don't be so quiet. Start yelling. Turn the TV up. Start arguing

6.  No, don't listen to the dentist. Candy and cookies are good for your teeth.

7. Yes, that Superdoopa Computer Game is too expensive but let's buy it anyway and we'll put it in your room.

8. What's that? You broke the kitchen window. Good!

9. Can someone go to the store for a newspaper? Here's $100; keep the change.

10. Yes, I know it's Monday, but why don't we stay home from school anyway?

Woof

Allan Ahlberg

Illustrated by Fritz Wegner

Eric first turned into a dog a little at a time in his own bed. His parents were downstairs watching television. His sister Emily was fast asleep in the next room. The time was ten past nine; the day, Wednesday; the month, May. Until then it had been a normal day for Eric. He'd done his paper-route with Roy, and gone to school. He'd had two helpings of his favorite dinner. He'd played with Emily before dinner, and Roy after. He'd watched television, had a shower, and gone to bed. Now he was *in* bed and turning into a dog.

It happened like this. Eric was lying on his side with his eyes closed. He was almost asleep. Suddenly, he felt an itch inside the collar of his pajama top. This—although he didn't know it yet—was the fur sprouting. He felt a curious tingling in his hands and feet. This was his hands and feet turning into paws. He felt his nose becoming cold and wet, his ears becoming floppy. Eric opened his eyes. He didn't panic right away. This was his nature, partly, but also he was still half-asleep. The thought in his mind was: "I'm turning into a dog!"

That was another thing about Eric: he was a good guesser. When Emily first learned to talk, it was usually Eric who guessed what she was trying to say. He could guess the mood his teacher was in, just from the way she held her attendance-book in the morning. Now—on the evidence of a furry paw where his hand should have been—he guessed he was turning into a dog. He didn't suppose he was turning into a werewolf, for instance, which is what Roy Ackerman would have thought. He didn't suppose he was dreaming, either, which he was not.

The time it took Eric to turn into a dog—his shape blurring and rippling like a swimmer under water—was about fifteen seconds. The time it took him to become frantic was about five seconds after that. His first action was to begin squirming in the bed, trying to get a better look at himself. His thoughts were in a turmoil: "I'm a dog! A *dog*!"

The next thing he did was try to get out of bed. This wasn't easy for a dog in pajamas; besides, they were baggy on him now. Eric leaped, and landed in a heap. He kicked his way clear of the trousers and backed out of the top. He resisted the urge to growl when one of his claws got caught in a buttonhole. He sat on the floor and thought: "I'm a dog!"

(Excerpt from *Woof* by Allan Ahlberg)

Cleaning My Room

Stephen Whiteside   Illustrated by Celina Mosbauer

Whenever I'm ordered to clean my room,

I never get rattled, I think with my head.

I fill every drawer

With junk from the floor.

I shove all the bigger stuff under the bed.

7

Reasons We Can't Get a Dog

Steven Herrick   *Illustrated by Mitch Vane*

SCRITCH
SCRITCH

We don't have a fence.

You wouldn't want him wandering off
onto the road, would you?

We have nowhere for him to sleep.

No, he couldn't sleep
on your brother Tom's bed.
All the snoring
would keep Tom awake.

We have nothing to feed him.

Yes, you could give him your vegetables,
but I don't think your mom would approve.

Besides, dogs scratch, bite, whimper,
howl at the moon.

Yes, I know your brother does, too,
but we can't take him to the pound, can we?

And do you want the dog chasing poor
Mrs. Sims and her cat down the road?

Yes, it would be funny.

But not for Mrs. Sims.

And don't say you have no one to play with.

What about me?

No, I won't fetch your ball,
roll over, or play dead!

Hmmm... Maybe we
should get a dog.

Digger Reckons

Don Carter

Illustrated by Craig Smith

Chapter One

I could hear the faint sounds of the *thwack!* of the tennis ball against the brick wall of the house. I crept around the corner. Lenny was trying out his new tennis racket.

I slunk along the fence partly hidden by the green leafy shrubs until I was behind Lenny. He hadn't seen me.

Charge! I sprinted at the wall as Lenny whacked the ball. I caught it on the first bounce, rushed around the side of the house, and hid behind the garbage can and some cardboard boxes. *Not bad for an old dog!* I complimented myself.

I could hear Lenny yelling, "I'll get you!" as he came racing up to the boxes, looking along the fenceline.

I was panting and tried to calm my breathing so that he wouldn't hear me.

"I'll find you," Lenny was saying, creeping and searching.

Suddenly, a hand thrust through the boxes and grabbed my collar. It dragged me onto the sidewalk.

"Got you!" said Lenny proudly.

He reached for a length of rope and threaded it through my collar. He tied the other end to the clothes line. He then wrapped his fingers around the tennis ball and pulled it from my mouth.

"Stay there!" he ordered, crankily.

Sometimes, I reckoned, *it was no fun being a dog.*

I closed my eyes and tried to think about other things to take my mind off the *thwack* of the tennis ball. When I heard movement nearby, I opened one eye and looked toward the fence.

Next door's cat! *Oh, please come closer!* I thought to myself. I watched the cat walk along the top of the fence. I tensed my muscles, ready to lunge at it.

Go! I scrambled to my feet and dashed to the fence, about to bark the loudest, most ferocious bark I could manage.

As I launched myself at the cat on the fence-top, the rope around my neck jerked tight and snapped me backward, into the dirt. My savage bark sounded like a frog croaking.

The cat paused to look down at me, then sprang gracefully into the neighbor's yard.

"Digger, you're a nut!" laughed Lenny, watching me.

A nut? I thought.

Sometimes being a dog was confusing, I reckoned.

Chapter Two

Lenny untied me later and went inside the house. I put my nose against the screen door. I could smell Lenny's tennis shoes nearby. *I might chew on those later on, if I get a chance,* I thought.

But what made my tongue hang out of my mouth and drip with delight was the delicious aroma of sizzling steak.

I sat up straight, ears pointed skyward, and tilted my head sideways.

"Don't worry, Digger," said Lenny's mom through the kitchen window, "we'll take care of you."

There are some things worth waiting for, I reckoned. I settled down to wait for the juicy steak bones.

Next door at Mrs. Eccleston's place, I heard rustling in the garden. She was watering the shrubs. I decided to surprise her. I might be getting old, but I was still proud of the smooth, silent way I could sneak up on someone. My paws padded across the yard to the gate. I squeezed my head through the posts.

This will make her jump, I chuckled to myself.

GRRRROOOOFF! GROOFF! I went berserk. Mrs. Eccleston shrieked and jumped two feet into the air with the hose aimed at the sky. She then swung around in my direction, the stream of water hitting me fully in the face.

Gasping, I squeezed my head back through the gate-posts. I heard the screen door opening and Mr. Eccleston comforting his wife.

But what really caught my attention was the sound of voices from inside the house. And the smell of a dog's natural enemy—the local dog catcher from the city pound. He was a short man with a belly that hung over his belt, and he always wore a sweat-stained, dirty shirt. He didn't catch many dogs—the smell of him approaching always gave him away.

I strained to hear the conversation inside. "The neighbors down the street have complained..." I could just hear him saying. "A dog has been making a nuisance of himself... I think it's your dog... he should be tied up... I need to take a look at him."

Chapter Three

He's talking about me! I thought. I had to act quickly. He was coming toward the screen door.

"Digger!" called Lenny and his mom as they approached the door.

"There he is!" said Lenny as he slid the door open.

Now was my chance!

I scurried in through the open door, past their grasping hands, and slid into the kitchen. I bumped into the small trash can which was full of garbage. A mix of delicious smells met my nose as fish bones, tuna oil, and lettuce scraps spilled over onto the white tiles. I struggled to my feet, and stepped in some spilled tomato sauce. The place looked like a garbage dump. Lenny stopped in shock.

"Oh, no! Digger, come here!" he gasped.

I sped into the living room leaving a trail of tomato-red paw prints across the floor. I felt the sauce on my feet squish as I ran across the carpet, straight into a table lamp. It rocked for a moment and then fell with a crash onto the glass coffee table. A magazine rack full of TV guides and newspapers fell sideways as I sprinted past.

I needed somewhere to hide—and quickly. The sounds of anger were coming closer as Lenny's mom led the chase holding my leash that she had grabbed from the back door. And I reckoned she wasn't going to take me to the park.

The curtains! They were the only place to hide. I lowered myself to my belly and crawled behind the couch and behind the curtains.

Suddenly it went very quiet. I heard Lenny trying to calm his mother, and craned my neck around the side of the couch to see him lead her back into the kitchen, his hand patting her on the shoulder in a comforting way. That just left the dog catcher—and I could smell him coming my way.

I tensed myself and decided that the best form of defense was attack. As he tiptoed toward me and leaned down to grab my collar, I snapped and snarled at him with the deepest, most threatening growl I could muster. He recoiled in fright, tripped over the coffee table, and fell backward into a vase of flowers. He had roses in his hair and threats in his eyes.

Lenny and his mom rushed back into the living room. I jumped out from behind the couch, taking the entire curtain with me, rod and all. The whole thing came crashing down as I ran toward the back door. Lenny's mom stared in disbelief, the dog catcher went even redder in the face, and I raced into the backyard.

I peered through the gate into the street and saw the dog catcher striding to his van, waving his arms as he talked to Lenny. He then slammed the van door and drove off with a screech.

Chapter Four

Being a dog catcher must be hard work, I reckoned. I sat waiting nervously at the back door. Lenny opened the door. He looked exhausted.

"Why do you have to make so much trouble, Digger? Mom is so angry with you," he said.

Then I noticed what he was carrying. He was holding a plate with those steak bones. *At last!*

"Sorry, Digger," continued Lenny, "I reckon after your performance inside, you don't deserve such a treat. And besides, we all reckon you're getting too fat!"

Lenny walked to the fence and emptied the plate into the other yard.

"The greyhounds will enjoy these," he muttered.

Lenny looked at me. I stared back. Surely, he could see the disbelief in my eyes.

"Look at this, Digger! Special weight-watcher's dog food from the vet! What do you reckon, eh?" he said as he dropped a handful of dry, brown pellets into my bowl.

What do I reckon? I wondered, as I gazed at my reflection in the glass sliding door.

I reckon your tennis shoes might get chewed tonight. And the next time I see that vet ...

Drawing Digger

Illustrator **Craig Smith**
talks to Jacquie Kilkenny about
illustrating *Digger Reckons...*
Photos by Kate Armstrong

Craig, when you were given the job of drawing Digger, how did you decide what kind of a dog he was going to be?

After reading the story, I knew he had to look a bit lean and mean. But I also wanted to give the impression that although he looked mean on the outside, he was really soft inside. I wanted him to be dusty, dirty colors. I also wanted him to have quite big ears, because dog's ears can show so much movement and expression, and this was important to convey some of Digger's emotions.

I think Digger is a great character—he is so knowing and sly, and sure of himself—I could really relate to him!

Your characters are nearly always funny looking, but in a gentle sort of way. When we look at them we want to laugh with them, not at them. Is this your intention?

Yes. I think what makes something funny is how characters respond to situations. That's where the humor is. Even when the story wants you to laugh at a character, it's better to turn it so we are laughing with them. I don't like making characters out to be too clownish or grotesque. It is funnier if you add the humor through body language and expression.

How do you decide on how a character should handle a situation and what their body language would be?

I read the story and think about what the character is like and how they would act and feel in certain situations. Sometimes I make faces or poses, and even act out a scene in front of the mirror so I can get a clear image in my mind, and then I can go and draw it. Acting in front of the mirror sometimes lets me see how funny certain expressions and body language can be. There can be a lot of humor in simple body language and expression. It doesn't have to be exaggerated.

How do you decide what each character should look like? Do they look like people you know?

How a character looks tends to just jump into my head—the people aren't strictly based on people I know, but more from a mixture of memories. For example, I don't know anyone who looks like the dog catcher, but he is like a blurred memory from childhood of what men from the local football club looked like.

Small details are important. I drew Lenny with messy hair on page 22 to show that he's a bit scruffy like Digger—they share some similar characteristics.

Now we know how you decide how characters look, but how do you actually decide what to draw?

The editor sends me copies of the text on the page, so I can see the space I have to fill, and this helps me to decide if I should do a close-up or a mid-shot. I usually try to illustrate the most humorous or dramatic part of the text on each page.

I start drawing basic shapes on the pages themselves, and see which ones work. I try to think of the story as a film, and what images could help to push it along.

I like it when you can flip through a book and get a strong sense of the story just from the illustrations.

For pages 12–13, there were lots of scenes I could have illustrated, but I thought it would be funny to show Digger being forced back by the leash—his plans failed, and feeling embarrassed, with the cat looking very smug.

I try to avoid drawing straight-out anger as anger on its own isn't funny. On page 20, the dog catcher is angry, but his body language is softened. The fact that the big and heavy man is trying hard to tiptoe, makes this illustration funnier.

For a number of illustrations, I chose to show only part of the people, so attention is focused on Digger. I also use this technique when I am drawing stories about babies and young children.

What makes you laugh?

It's hard to work out exactly what I laugh at. I laugh at obvious silliness. I laugh at jokes about going bald. But I also find a lot of humor in deceit—I laugh at knowing, sly characters... like Digger...

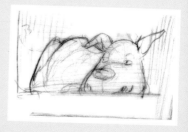

The Dangerous Dinosaur

Stephen Whiteside Illustrated by Ian Forss

If you stand very close to a dinosaur,
There's a very good chance you might die.
But it isn't the size of his mouth or his jaw,
And it isn't the look in his eye.

And it isn't his tail, so strong and so thick—
One swipe and you're mush or you're muck.
And it isn't his claws flashing past you so quick,
Or the fact that he's built like a truck.

No, it's something you can't really see with your eyes
That is likely to bring on your death.
The reason why walking up close isn't wise,
Is his terrible, horrible breath.

The smell is so bad, it's like old rotten meat,

It hits you as if it were brick.

It starts at your head, and it flows to your feet,

And you're soon feeling dizzy and sick.

So…

If with this problem you ever are faced,

Just hold your breath and be strong.

Bring a fire truck filled to the top with toothpaste,

And a toothbrush twenty feet long!

The School Play

Lilith Norman   *Illustrated by Virginia Barrett*

I was never cut out to be an actor.

But Jason was. He galloped around the house uttering his line in every possible way. "*Follow* the yellow brick road." "Follow the *yellow* brick road." "Follow the yellow brick *road*."

"Which do you think sounds best?" he asked us in turn. But since each of us gave him a different answer, we didn't help him much.

On the morning of the play, I felt dreadful. I knew I wouldn't be able to utter a word up there on that stage. I poked my cornflakes listlessly around the bowl, but my throat was too tight to eat.

"Come on," said Mom. "You'll be late for school. Eat up."

"I feel sick," I said.

"Nonsense!" said Mom. "You're just a bit nervous."

My sister Lee said, "Don't worry, David. All the great actors have butterflies in their stomachs before they go on stage. It helps them give a better performance. You'll see. Once you get out on the stage tonight you'll be fine."

School was pretty much a write-off that day, since everyone was so keyed up about the play. When I got home, Jason was wandering about near the fruit trees, and I could hear little bits of words floating back as he worked on his line for the zillionth time. "Follow... road... yellow... brick..."

Mom had me put our costumes and props in the car. By the time I gathered everything together it was supper time and she sent me out to find Jason.

He wasn't anywhere.

I called and called. Nothing. I walked down to the creek, and there was Jason. He was moaning and clutching his stomach. He was green.

"Ohh," he said. "I feel sick."

"Serves you right for stuffing yourself down here in the orchard. Anyway, Mom wants you. It's supper time."

Jason moaned again, and I looked at what he had been eating.

"Where did you get that meat from?" I asked.

"It isn't meat," wailed Jason. "It's...it's... caterpillars."

"CATERPILLARS!"

"I wanted butterflies in the stomach, too," said Jason. "But I couldn't catch any. So I thought maybe if I ate some caterpillars they'd hatch out in time..."

(Excerpt from *My Simple Little Brother* by Lilith Norman)

Funny Business

Have you ever wondered about the animals you see in TV shows, movies, and commercials? Do you think they might have been to acting school, or do you think that they are just someone's pet? Christine Powell knows the answer to these questions because she runs a casting agency for animals called "Animal Actors."

Casting the right animal

TV producers often call Christine when they want a cat or a dog—or maybe even a tiger or an elephant—to act in one of their shows. A producer might phone a day or two before an animal is wanted and say, "I need a golden labrador for Thursday at 10:00 a.m." Or even, "We need three elephants out at the High Ridge Shopping Center next week."

Where does Christine get all these animals from at such short notice? Unlike most casting agencies, she lives with a lot of the actors that are on her lists! Christine has a small farm, which is home to one emu, six dogs, six cats, two geese, one ferret, ten black pigs, one galah, and one blue-tongue lizard.

So, often when Christine gets a phone call, she knows she can supply the animal right away. But, if it is something unusual like a tiger, then Christine has to make a few phone calls.

Training animal actors

Many of the animal actors Christine has on her lists **are** people's pets who have been trained at an obedience school. Christine runs a weekly school for animals where they are taught to obey simple orders, like "sit" and "walk." Each animal must complete both a basic and advanced obedience course before they are eligible for acting jobs.

Good behavior for an animal actor is vital. Filming is very expensive. The quicker a scene is "shot," the better. If an animal misbehaves while being filmed on set, the scene must be done again, and the film producer can get very annoyed.

One time, Polly the galah, started saying "Hello, Hello," during a kissing scene for a television show. Polly had to be taken off the set and put into her cage until she settled down.

Make-up and special effects

Next time you are watching a show that has a wild animal in it, take a closer look. Because not many wild animals are animal actors, sometimes a producer has to use a trained animal wearing make-up and costume pieces.

Christine once had to provide a 'fox' at short notice. She found a corgi dog and attached a bushy tail. Then the dog was colored orangey-red with make-up.

There is a well-known saying, "Never work with children or animals." But Christine wouldn't have it any other way. She has been working with animals for twenty-eight years (and sometimes with children, too). Perhaps one day there will be an Academy Award for animal actors! And the winner is...

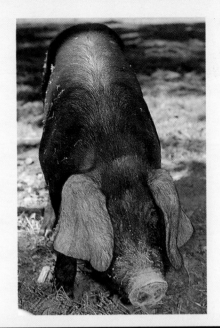

Finding the right animal for a part

Christine was asked recently to supply a cat actor for a children's television show. The cat required for the script had to be young, sleek, and black. The scene was to be set in a

lighthouse, and the cat was going to have to run up the curved staircase of the lighthouse.

Christine didn't have the kind of cat the script required, so she called Margaret and Rachel Parth, proud owners of Jet, a one-year-old cat.

It was Jet's first acting assignment. What follows is a day in the life of Jet, the animal actor... ⇨   ⇨   ⇨

A day in the life of Jet, cat actor

Why are you waking me up, Margaret? For a TV show? You know I don't watch TV.

Still, a girl has to eat.

8:00 a.m.

8:30 a.m.

Here I am arriving at the studio with Christine. Look at the door of the truck—it's a limo for animal actors. Where's Margaret?

We've been waiting so long and finally Nathan is checking me in.

10:00 a.m.

10:30 a.m.

They want me to sit up. OK. I'll do it! Lights! Camera! Action!

Here I go again…

And again!

3:32 p.m.

3:35 p.m.

3:40 p.m.

Magnetic Madness

Heather Hammonds *Illustrated by Stephen Axelsen*

Chapter One

"Thomas Williams, behave yourself!" shouted the teacher.

Tom's class was on a field trip to the Science Museum, and he had just borrowed a helmet from one of the space suits on display.

"Sorry, Mrs. Woods," he said, putting it back. "It's those vitamin bars I've been eating; they give me so much energy that I can't stop."

Tom's mom had bought a box of fruit bars for him. They were full of vitamins and minerals, but there was an awful lot of sugar in them, too …

Tom's friend Richard thought that Tom's bad behavior was very funny. So far, Tom had changed the astronomy model so that the sun went around the earth; he'd mixed up all the trash in the recycling display; and even managed to switch off all the lights in the middle of the sound and light show, without getting caught.

"Here is a special exhibit," said Mrs. Woods, leading the class over to a roped-off area. "These machines are called Magnetic Field Generators."

Two large machines stood opposite each other, and sitting between them was a block of metal.

"When I pull this lever, these generators will magnetize this block of iron," Mrs. Woods explained. "Then other pieces of metal will stick to it."

Tom winked at Richard and sneaked under the rope. Just as the teacher pulled the lever, he ran between the machines.

"Ta-da! I'm magnetized!" he yelled.

Everybody laughed, except Mrs. Woods.

"People can't be magnetized," she said. "I've had enough of you; go and sit in the bus with Mrs. Peabody until it's time for us to leave."

Feeling rather silly, Tom did as he was told.

Chapter Two

It was lunch time when the class arrived back at school, and everyone went to eat their lunch except Tom, who had to go to the classroom.

"Why can't you behave?" asked Mrs. Woods, tapping away at her brand new computer as he stood in front of her desk. "Reports are being sent home soon, and I'm thinking of giving you a poor one. What are we going to do with you?"

All at once, the computer made a loud sizzling noise. Tom leaned forward to see what was wrong and the computer's screen suddenly went bright green. Then, in a puff of smoke, it blew up.

"Oh, no!" Mrs. Woods wailed. "Go to lunch, and I'll deal with you later."

Tom scratched his head as he left the room, and a few paper clips dropped out of his hair. Somehow they had found their way off the desk and onto his head. He began to wonder if people could be magnetized after all ...

Chapter Three

After lunch, the students filed into the classroom and took their seats.

"Look at Lucy—she's staring at you," whispered Richard, who was sitting next to Tom.

Lucy Sawyer sat across the aisle from the boys. Everyone knew that Lucy liked Tom a lot, and Richard even called her Tom's "girlfriend" sometimes, just to annoy him. Lucy wore braces and they glinted in the light, as she leaned toward Tom with a weird smile on her face.

"Help!" he cried, as she suddenly flew out of her seat and stuck her mouth on his neck.

The whole class began to laugh.

"She's **kissing** you," snickered Richard.

"She's a **vampire**," shouted Tom. "She's biting me!"

"Lucy, control yourself!" said a shocked Mrs. Woods.

But poor Lucy couldn't. She was stuck to Tom's neck, and he had to push her away.

"I didn't mean it," she muttered, rubbing her lips. "My braces started aching and then ... pow!"

Tom was very embarrassed.

A few minutes later, Richard slapped his arm.

"Sorry, Tom, it's my watch," he said. "It keeps trying to ... stick to you."

With a sinking feeling, Tom realized that he really **was** magnetized.

Tom spent the rest of the day picking things off his sweater and out of his hair. Paper clips, a pencil sharpener, staples, and even someone's keys. At last it was time to go home, and he and Richard raced from the schoolground.

"Where are we going?" asked Richard.

"To visit my grandma," Tom replied. "She might be able to help me."

Tom's grandma was a scientist, and she was the smartest person he knew.

Chapter Four

Grandma frowned, when Tom told her the whole story.

"We will have to do a test," she sighed.

She made him lie down on his back on her shiny kitchen floor.

"Point your arms and make your body like an arrow," she said. "Let's see if you spin around and point to the north, like a compass."

Slowly Tom's body began to turn, until he was indeed pointing North.

"Wow!" chuckled Richard, poking Tom with his foot to make him spin again. "You'd never get lost!"

"It's not funny," moaned Tom.

"You're definitely magnetized," said Grandma. "I'll see if I can find a way to solve this problem."

The boys watched cartoons while Grandma read some science books. Tom made sure he didn't sit too close to the television, in case he wrecked it.

"I've got it!" Grandma finally exclaimed. "Heat!"

49

"Heat?" asked Tom.

"Go and take a hot bath," Grandma said. "Iron is demagnetized by heating it in a furnace, but you're only a boy, so a hot bath should do. Go on; you can use my lavender bubble bath if you want."

"No thanks," scowled Tom, heading off to Grandma's bathroom.

Chapter Five

Tom soon returned, looking pink and clean.

"Let's see if it worked," he said to Richard.

Carefully, Richard put his watch near Tom. Nothing happened. Then Tom stood beside the television set. It didn't go green or sizzle at all.

"I'm back to normal!" he cheered. "I'll never goof around on school field trips again."

"And I'd give up those fruit bars, too, if I were you," laughed Grandma.

FRUIT

Graeme Parsons   Illustrated by Alex Tyers

The apples started it. "We're cold." "Everyone stares at us." "They pick us up." "Then they put us down."

In the next display, the bananas began to complain. "If we're green, they say we're too hard." "If we're yellow, they say we're too soft."

The strawberries listened.

"I'm dying for a bit of sunshine," sighed one of the older apricots.

"Me too," responded a juicy peach.

"We've been here too long," said the fattest banana. "It's more like a jail than a supermarket."

The other fruit agreed—especially the grapes, who were missing the leafy vines of home. "Let's go!" all the fruit yelled.

"But where?" asked the peach.

"Anywhere!" snapped an apple crisply.

Just then, Tanya the stock girl came by.

"Hey Tanya!" called the banana. "Get us out of here!"

It was the first time Tanya had been spoken to by fruit. She scratched her head.

"Put us in a basket and take us out!" the banana continued. "You work here. No one will stop you."

Tanya considered the banana's request.

"Please!" pleaded the grapes.

"Right," said Tanya. "I'll do it."

"All of us, all of us!" cried the fruit.

Tanya grabbed as much fruit as she could—bananas, apples, apricots, peaches, strawberries, grapes, kiwi fruit, oranges, and lemons. The basket was nearly full.

Among the vegetables, a tomato had seen what was happening. "Take me too," it called. The mushrooms murmured. A cucumber waved. The potatoes bumped one another. The onions cried. An excited garlic clove fell on the floor.

Tanya picked up the noisy vegetables and put them in the basket. She grabbed some other vegetables, too. Then she saw her boss coming. Tanya put her head down and hurried through the back exit, as her boss called out, "Glad to see you're getting rid of the damaged items, Tanya."

"We're not damaged—thank you very much," muttered the fruit and vegetables to Tanya.

Once outside, Tanya looked both ways as traffic whizzed past. *What next?* she thought.

"Let's go to the beach!" suggested a strawberry.

"Great idea! Take us to the beach, Tanya," said the fat banana. He liked telling Tanya what to do.

On the bus ride, the fruit and vegetables kept very quiet, especially when an old man stared oddly at them. A boy asked Tanya if he could have a peach. She said "no" and all the fruit breathed a sigh of relief.

As Tanya walked down the steps from the bus stop to the beach, she held the basket carefully. She put it down on the soft, white sand.

"We're here, we're here!" squealed the grapes.

Tanya sat down and yawned. "This is too strange. I don't even want to think about why I'm here and why I'm listening to a banana."

"Don't go to sleep," said the fat banana. "Not while we're stuck here!"

Tanya was getting sick of being bossed around by fruit. She tipped the basket onto its side, then she rolled over and closed her eyes.

The fruit and vegetables tumbled out. Several grapes were squashed by a sweet potato. The apricot got a nasty bruise when an orange landed on her. The cucumber rolled over the garlic clove and complained about the smell. But everyone else was fine.

"Let's go!" shouted the strawberries, rolling across the sand.

The garlic clove ran after the strawberries and everyone else followed—except for the lemons, who were sour at the best of times.

The waves lapped the shore. Curved shells sparkled in the sun. The strawberries rolled into the shells and bobbed about in the shallow waves. The grapes cheered and rolled into the water. The carrot dived in after them and splashed about in the shallows.

The potatoes were happy on the sand. They had found a seaweed pod that was happy to be used for a football. They bumped one another and fell over. Some kiwi fruit rolled past happily playing football.

The banana lay down at the water's edge. He remembered his family swaying among tropical fronds. (They had been a close bunch.) The oranges lay in a hollow, sunning themselves. Passionfruit danced with mushrooms in the shallows while the lemons made bitter comments.

The garlic clove paddled on some seaweed into deep water. Then she dived off and let the waves carry her back. On the way, she bumped into an onion. "You stink," they said to each other. Then they burst out laughing.

The apricot and the peach had found a shady spot. They sat beside one another and compared bruises.

The apples looked on, feeling pleased. "If it hadn't been for us..."

"May I join you?" asked the sweaty green cucumber.

Fruit and vegetables were everywhere—swimming, playing, lazing, chatting.

Then Tanya woke up. "Hey! We have to go back! My lunch hour is nearly over, and you'll all be ruined."

She was right. The day was getting hot. The fat banana knew it best. He was feeling mushy inside. Quickly, he helped Tanya to round up the others. A few grapes were missing. "We'll have to leave them," said Tanya.

Everyone felt sorry, but they knew the grapes had gone happily.

It was early afternoon when they got back to the supermarket. Just before Tanya put the fruit and vegetables back in their displays, the banana spoke up. "There are just two things I'd like to say," he told the surprised stock girl. "First, thank you from all of us."

All the fruit clapped together.

"And second," he continued, "later on today, when people complain that we look tired—which they always do—at least we'll know there's a good reason why. And for the first time we'll be happy to hear it."

All the fruit laughed. They were glad they'd been picked.

Buster and the Balloon Man

Illustrated by Chantal Stewart

The balloon man came down our street every Monday night at exactly six o'clock. He was never late and never early. Just as the big hand was up, and the little hand was down, on every clock in every house in every street, we could see the balloon man coming slowly down from the park, with his brightly-colored balloons.

It was fun waiting for him to arrive. Sometimes we played hide-and-seek around the lamppost. Sometimes we played hopscotch, and other times we just sat around making up our minds which color balloon we would buy.

Buster was a fat little bulldog that lived at Ross McKay's house. He didn't like anyone to come near the house. Instead of running and playing like the other dogs in the street, Buster just sat on the front steps and waited for someone to come along so he could growl and chase them.

Buster didn't like the balloon man, and the balloon man didn't like Buster. When Buster growled at him, the balloon man would run back up the street to the park where there were "no dogs allowed." Buster would go back to his step and wait for someone else to come along.

Luckily for us we lived at the end of the street near the park. We got to the balloon man before Buster did. The children from down the street always ran to meet him, that is, all the children but one little girl named Janie.

Janie had been sick and couldn't walk very well, much less run. Every Monday she waited and waited, hoping that the nasty bulldog would let the balloon man get down to her house, but it never worked out. Sometimes we would buy a balloon for Janie. She always smiled and said, "Thank you," but we knew she wanted to join in the fun of choosing. Never once did Buster let the balloon man near Janie's house.

Not until that special Monday night! That night everything seemed the same. As usual we were waiting for the balloon man to arrive. Some of us were playing hopscotch. Some were playing around the lamppost and shouting, "Here I come, ready-or-not."

In all the houses on the street, clocks began to chime, ring, cuckoo, and tick six o'clock. Then we saw the balloon man coming from the park. He didn't look any different. He had on his same blue coat, and his same old straw hat, and he carried a lot of brightly colored balloons. He was walking slowly as he always did, so we could take our time choosing. We always changed our minds about a hundred times. First we'd pick a red balloon, then change it for a green one, and then ask for a yellow one like the one somebody else had. But the balloon man never became annoyed with us. He seemed to know that choosing was half the fun.

As the balloon man came nearer, we noticed there was something different. He had balloons all right, but they weren't on sticks as they usually were. They were tied to the ends of strings that were standing straight up in the air. It was magic! Everybody could see it was magic.

Buster growled in his usual way and started after the balloon man. This time the balloon man didn't run. He stood his ground and looked down at the little white bulldog. He took a short fat stick out of his pocket and fastened a balloon to it. Buster grabbed the stick and, because he was a bulldog, pulled and pulled on it. He held on to it for dear life. Then it happened. The balloon man let go of the stick, and the balloon took off into space.

"Oh!" we all cried. "Look at Buster. He's going up like a helicopter."

Ross began to cry. Although Buster was nasty, he was still Ross's dog. Mothers and fathers came out of their houses, down from their porches and out from backyards.

The little fat dog went higher and higher, and finally the wind blew him behind some trees and out of sight.

The balloon man didn't say a word. He just let us take longer than usual to choose our balloons. When he arrived at Janie's house, he sat on her steps and let her pick her own balloon. Janie was just like the rest of us. She changed her mind from red to blue and green. Then finally she asked for a yellow one.

The next day was just another Tuesday for most people, but not on our street. Everyone was up very early looking for Buster and the runaway balloon.

But Buster was back. There he was, sitting in his usual place on Ross McKay's steps. But somehow he was different. When the newspaper girl came to deliver the paper, Buster didn't bark. When the mailman came to deliver the mail, Buster didn't growl. When the street cleaners drove past, Buster didn't even raise his head.

The next Monday night when the clocks began to chime, ring, cuckoo, and tick six o'clock, Buster dropped his ears and went under the front steps. The balloon man came along, and everyone, even Janie, had time to choose a balloon. It was a Monday night we will never forget.

If you ever see a balloon flying through the air with a dog holding on to it, don't be surprised. It could be another nasty dog like Buster, learning a lesson from the balloon man.